Norman the Naughty Knight

and the

Flying Horse

For Sir Rafi the Royal and Sir Tom the Tremendous,
tellers of terrific tales – S . P-H .

For Finnley and Jocelyn, my little knights – I . S .

EGMONT
We bring stories to life

Book Band: Purple

First published in Great Britain 2017
by Egmont UK Ltd
The Yellow Building, 1 Nicholas Road, London W11 4AN
Text copyright © Smriti Prasadam-Halls 2017
Illustrations copyright © Ian Smith 2017
The author and illustrator have asserted their moral rights.
ISBN 978 1 4052 8453 0
www.egmont.co.uk
A CIP catalogue record for this title is available from the British Library.
Printed in Singapore.
65129/1

Stay safe online. Any website addresses listed in this book are correct at the time of going to print.
However, Egmont is not responsible for content hosted by third parties. Please be aware that
online content can be subject to change and websites can contain content that is unsuitable for
children. We advise that all children are supervised when using the internet.

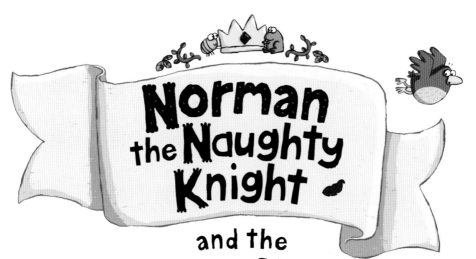

Norman the Naughty Knight
and the
Flying Horse

WITHDRAWN

Smriti Prasadam-Halls
Illustrated by Ian Smith

Reading Ladder

Norman Knight was very excited.
There was going to be a jousting
contest at Creaky Castle.

Everyone was busy getting ready.

King Harold was tooting his trumpet,
Queen Betsy was practising her speech,
Prince Henry was shining his sword,
Cook was cooking jelly, Doris the
dragon was cleaning the chimneys
and Norman . . .

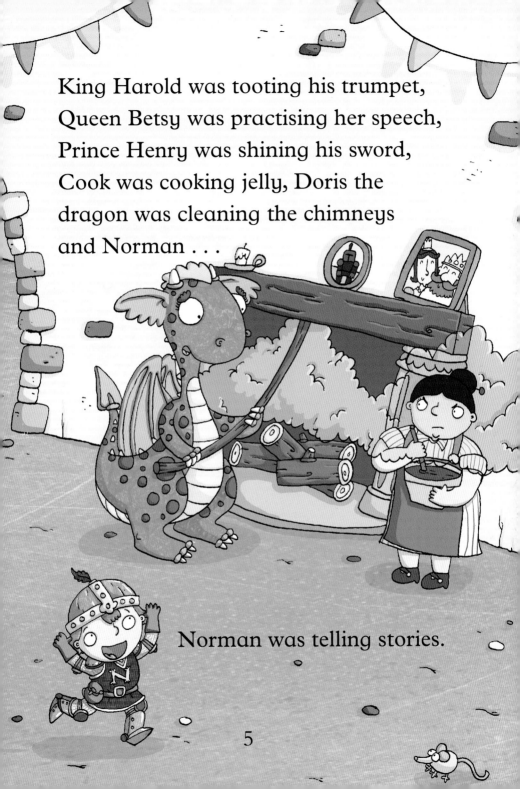

Norman was telling stories.

Norman loved telling all sorts of stories.

Funny ones, like this . . .

'I could
ride a
horse
upside
down!'

Silly ones,
like this . . .

'I could
fight with my
hands behind
my back!'

And CRAZY ones, like this . . .

'I could win any jousting
contest in the world!'

Luckily, if he ever got TOO carried away with his stories, his pet dragon, Doris, would sit on him.

Like this.

Ouch!

As the day of the jousting contest got nearer Doris found herself sitting on Norman A LOT.

Norman wasn't taking part in the joust because all the places were taken, but he liked to talk about it.

'It's such a shame,' he said cheekily. 'I wanted to show everyone my super jousting skills!'

On the first evening of the joust there was a feast to welcome the knights. Everyone gathered in the Banqueting Hall.

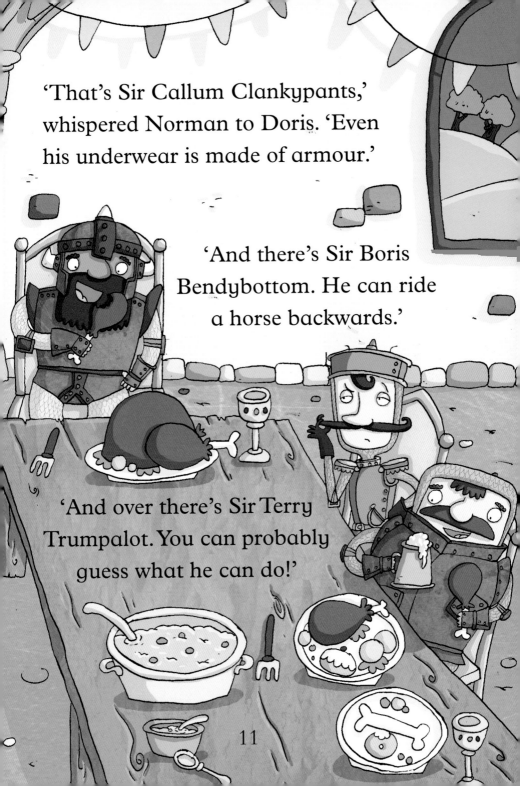

'That's Sir Callum Clankypants,' whispered Norman to Doris. 'Even his underwear is made of armour.'

'And there's Sir Boris Bendybottom. He can ride a horse backwards.'

'And over there's Sir Terry Trumpalot. You can probably guess what he can do!'

11

Just then a very tall knight entered the hall.

Everything went quiet.

'Who's THAT?' asked Doris.

'That's the Red Knight,' whispered Norman. 'No one has ever defeated him.'

After the knights had eaten as much
creaky casserole and jousting jelly as they
wanted, they gathered next to the fire
to tell stories. Some of them told stories
about famous knights. Some of them told
stories about wonderful weapons.

13

Soon it was Norman's turn.

'Did you ever hear the story of the Headless Horseman?' asked Norman, mysteriously.

'H-h-headless H-h-horseman?' stuttered Sir Terry Trumpalot. 'Oh yes,' said Norman naughtily, 'he's been spotted riding round this way!'

Norman went on. 'And of course there's the Ghost of Creaky Castle.'

'G-g-ghost?' whispered Sir Terry.

'Oh yes,' said Naughty Norman. 'Listen out for him tonight!'

'And then there's the Flying Horse that . . .'

By now Sir Terry's teeth were chattering. 'F-f-flying horse?'

'Oh yes,' said Norman, 'they say his enormous wings can . . .'

'Well, I don't believe a word!' cut in Sir Boris Bendybottom haughtily.

'Me neither,' said Sir Callum Clankypants, standing up, but looking a tiny bit worried.

15

'Norman!' said the queen crossly.
'That's quite enough of your stories. Off
to bed with you!'

'Ouch!' said Norman, peering out
from underneath Doris. 'Sorry Mum,
I thought everyone would enjoy a nice
bedtime story!'

The next morning King Harold rushed in with some bad news.

'Sir Terry has dropped out of the contest.' He moaned. 'We don't have enough knights for the competition now. Whatever shall we do?'

'Bad luck, Dad,' said Norman, munching a slice of tournament toast.

'Maybe Norman can take Sir Terry's place?' said his brother Henry with a twinkle in his eye. 'He could show us his skills!'

'WHAT? Erm, no – I'm very BUSY today!' protested Norman. 'I've got . . . erm, stuff . . . erm . . . to do.'

'That's a brilliant idea!' said the king, marching off to spread the good news.

'Yeah, Norman,' said Henry. 'Now you can show us how it's really done!'

18

Norman was horrified. He had absolutely no idea how to joust. It was just a silly story.

'Don't worry, Norman,' said Doris, 'I'll help you.'

'Thanks, Doris,' said Norman, cheering up a bit. 'Let's do some practice. I mean how hard can it REALLY be?'

The answer was VERY hard indeed.

First you had to ride your horse really fast without falling off.

Then you had to ride your horse really fast and wave your lance in the air at the same time, without falling off.

And THEN you had to ride your horse really fast, wave your lance in the air and knock the other person over all at the same time, without falling off.

Uh-oh!

Norman and Doris practised all morning, but it was no use. Norman simply couldn't get the hang of it.

'Cheer up!' said Doris, pulling Norman out of the moat AGAIN. 'You'll be fine.'

But she didn't look at all sure about that.

Just then Cook appeared, panting.
'What are you doing here, Norman?
Everyone's looking for you on the field.
The contest has started. It's your turn!'

'Oh no!' groaned Norman.

He arrived at the field just in time for his first joust.

Norman quickly put his helmet on. He put his boots on. And he was just putting his armour on when the trumpet tooted.

'Let the games begin!' called the king.

'Wait! I'm not ready!' cried Norman.

But it was too late. Sir Boris
Bendybottom was charging
right at him.

Norman's horse galloped on to the field, but Norman couldn't see a thing. His helmet was trapped inside his armour. He tried to push his head out but it was stuck.

'Argh!' shouted Norman.

Then he heard another shout. It came from Sir Boris.

'Help! It's the Headless Horseman! He's coming to get me!'

'Where? Where is he?' said Norman, finally pushing his head through and peering out, but Sir Boris had run off the field crying, 'Help! Help! The Headless Horseman!'

'That was a lucky escape!' giggled Norman. He had a little rest while some of the other knights were jousting.

He watched closely, trying to pick up some tips, but very soon the trumpet was tooting again. It was time for Round Two.

'At least you've got your armour on this time!' said Doris.

'Let's go, Ned!' said Norman to his horse. 'Gee up!'

But Norman's horse had other ideas. Ned had spotted a squirrel and began to trot after it, towards the castle.

'No! No!' said Norman, pulling on the reins, but nothing was going to stop Ned. He galloped into the courtyard, past the kitchen and straight through the washing line!

Norman was soon tangled in a white
sheet. 'HELP!' he yelled, as Ned charged
after the squirrel and back on to the field.

'Woooahh!' he shrieked, trying not to
fall off.

Then Norman heard another shriek.

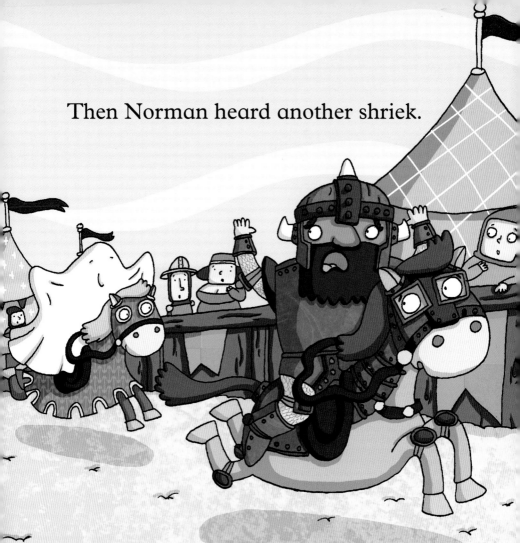

It came from Sir Callum Clankypants.
'Help! It's the Ghost of Creaky Castle!
He's REAL!'

And Sir Callum rode off the field as fast
as he could howling, 'I want my mama!'

'I'm not a ghost!' called Norman, untangling himself at last, but Sir Callum was out of sight.

'This jousting contest isn't too bad after all,' Norman said to Doris. 'I can't believe I've made it to The Final!'

Then he saw his last opponent.

Norman
gulped.

Doris
gulped.

Norman's
horse took
one look
and bolted.

'What am I going to do?' wailed Norman.
'I've got to face THE RED KNIGHT
and I don't even have a horse!'

Doris rolled her eyes. 'Now, I do NOT
think this is a good idea . . .' she grumbled,
'but I suppose I shall have to be
your horse. Just this once.'

Norman gave Doris a big hug.

The trumpet tooted. It was time for The Final. Norman and Doris rode on to the field.

'Ho ho! What a funny little knight!
Ha ha! What a funny-looking horse!'
roared the Red Knight.

'I shall knock you down in a flash!'
He raised his lance and thundered
towards them.

Closer and closer he galloped.

'Oh no!' cried Norman.

'Oh help!' moaned Doris.

The Red Knight had almost reached them.

Norman shut his eyes tightly.

The Red Knight kept riding.

Doris kept riding.

They got closer and closer . . .

. . . until there was only one thing for
it. Doris did what any sensible dragon-
pretending-to-be-a-horse would do . . .

She flapped her great big dragon wings and FLEW over the Red Knight.

The Red Knight was so astonished
to see a flying horse that he galloped
straight into a tree, fell off his horse and
landed on his head in a ditch.

The crowd went wild. 'Hooray!
Hooray for Norman and his
Flying Horse!' they cheered.

That evening there was an enormous feast. 'Well done to Norman, winner of the joust!' said the king and queen proudly. 'Super horse skills! Amazing stunts!'

'Not bad, little brother,' chuckled Prince
Henry.

'Well I did have a little help from a
friend!' said Norman winking at Doris.

'A LITTLE help?' snorted Doris, and
she sat on Norman with a big squelch.

Creaky Castle still holds a jousting contest every year. Knights come from far and wide to show off their skills.

They ride, they joust, they feast and they tell stories.

Some stories are about famous knights and some stories are about wonderful weapons . . .

. . . but everyone's FAVOURITE story is the one about Norman Knight and his amazing Flying Horse.